SIMON & SCHUSTER
Rockefeller Center
1230 Avenue of the Americas
New York, NY 10020

SIMON & SCHUSTER and colophon are registered trademarks of Simon & Schuster, Inc.

Designed by Mark Wasserman and Irene Ng of Plinko.

Manufactured in Singapore.

10 9 8 7 6 5 4 3 2 1

Library of Congress Cataloging-in-Publication Data is available.

Published by the HOW Series, Dedicated to the Exploration and Dissemination of Unbelievable Brilliance.
The HOW Series is a division of the Brutus Blue Publishing Force, which is a division of McSweeney's Publishing, which is located on Earth.

Photographs of Dr. and Mr. Haggis-On-Whey by Meiko Arquillos.
Photographs on pp. 25, 26, and 29 by John Wasserman of Wasser-shot Images.
Cover illustration by Michael Kupperman.
Giraffe Illustrations on pp. 21, 32, and 37 by Peter Gray.
Illustration on p. 7 by Robert Fenn.
Additional design elements by Eric Baldwin.

All rights are reserved, except the right to wear orange and brown together, which we leave to you people who do that kind of thing. Permission to reprint this book in whole or part is prohibited, unless your name is Myron. We love people named Myron. If you can prove that your name is Myron, then we allow you to do anything you want with this book. You can use it for insulation, you can make wedding dresses from it. Up to you. If you are not named Myron, you are permitted only to read this book and to set up a shrine in a corner of your home where you may worship this book. You may read it eleven times, BUT NO MORE! More than eleven times can be very dangerous. Take our word on that. This boy, shown at right, read a previous work of ours twelve times and suffered the consequences you see. So be smart about this! Eleven times only. Pace yourself.

Acknowledgments hereby are directed to Mr. D.H., Mr. M.C., Abraham Lincoln (who urged us to publish our findings — thanks, Abe!), Sergei Vlamikov [first man to wear a spacesuit (he was a model, not a Cosmonaut)], Ms. V.V., and, most of all, the nation of Denmark. Thank you for the tulips and the color ochre. Hail Danes, and their delicious fish desserts!

The authors also wish to grudgingly acknowledge these earlier works, which may have had a minor influence upon our own infinitely more impressive work:
Charles and Dixie Newcastle, *Giraffes in the Home*
Hamilton Jefferson, *Heroes of the Animal Kingdom*
Craig Fontaigne, *Aborigines in 18th Century Russia*
Abe Stilberg, *Outliving Caesar: The Giraffe Boy-Prince Quaddus*
Terry Jacobson, *The Alpha Giraffe and the Cost-Effective Green Rollercoaster*

www.haggis-on-whey.com
www.mcsweeneys.net

ISBN 0-7432-6726-5

For information regarding special discounts for bulk purchases, please contact Simon & Schuster Special Sales at 1-800-456-6798 or business@simonandschuster.com

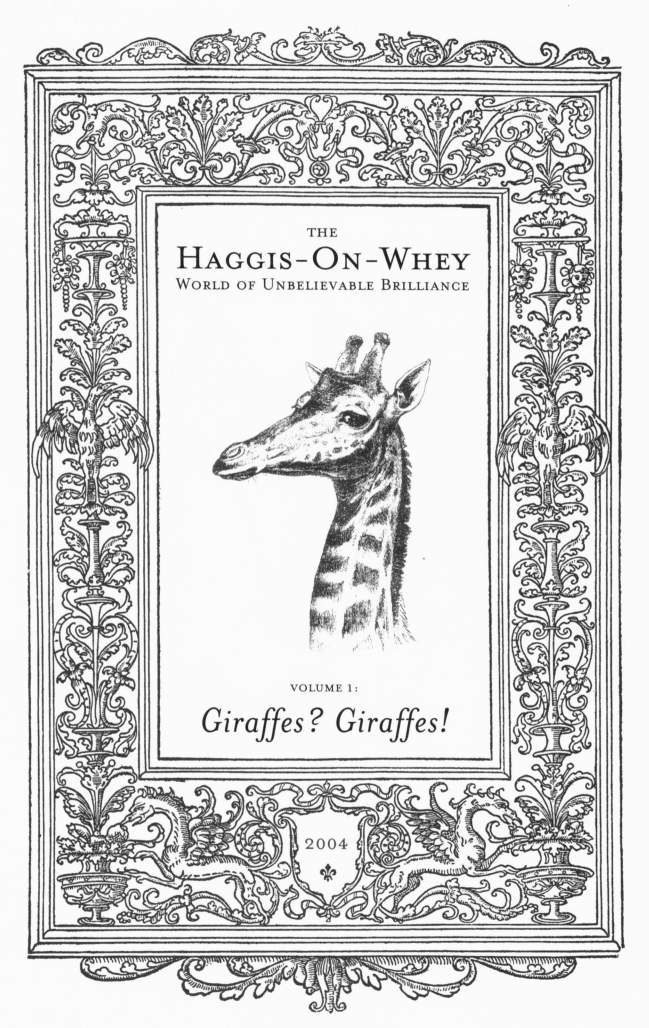

THE
HAGGIS-ON-WHEY
WORLD OF UNBELIEVABLE BRILLIANCE

VOLUME 1:

Giraffes? Giraffes!

2004

SIMON & SCHUSTER

New York London Toronto Sydney

DR. AND MR. DORIS HAGGIS-ON-WHEY'S WORLD OF UNBELIEVABLE BRILLIANCE

Greetings. I am Dr. Doris Haggis-On-Whey, the world-famous scientist and explorer you have heard so much about. The man standing next to me is my husband, Benny. He helps me with my work, and tells adequate knock-knock jokes. I am glad that you have picked up this book. It shows that you are someone who looks to discover new things, and who, like me, dislikes hummus.

For the past forty years, my husband Benny and I have traveled the globe, collecting information and writing down our findings. It is my opinion that our findings are the most important and startling scientific information known to humankind. If you disagree with me, you are wrong.

Mr. Haggis-On-Whey and I live in a county called Crumpets-Under-Kilt, on the distant Isle of Air, in the northernmost reaches of Scotland. It is here that we store all of our equipment and our maps, rare animals, and scientific findings. For forty years all our information was kept very secret, until recently, when we decided to share our findings with the world, with common people, with good and smart people, and even people like you.

And so was born the Haggis-On-Whey series of Unbelievable Brilliance, by far the most comprehensive and impressive series of reference books yet written by humankind. This book about the storied and mysterious world of giraffes is the first in the series, which will soon enough number in the hundreds and will include books about: Wolverines, Hallways, Neptune, Dogs Who Play Poker, Cardboard, Giant Squids, The Post Office, Thrones, Lunch Boxes, Garbage, Teeth, and Chartreuse.

Please observe the following rules when reading these books:

1) Wash your filthy hands.

2) Wash your filthy face.

3) If one is available, put on a red vest.

4) Do not drink anything orange or yellow within two hours of opening this book.

5) Do not lick your fingers before turning the pages. I don't care if you've just washed them.

Now, onward into the World of Unbelievable Brilliance.

Dr. and Mr. Doris Haggis-On-Whey

We are here to learn about giraffes, or GIRAFFES. Giraffes are animals, sometimes known as aminals. A definition: Aminal (optional: animal): a being or creature that walks or flies and eats food. Aminals usually inhabit the Earth, roaming and looking at this and that and chewing cud or gum, but can sometimes inhabit your body cavities, where it is dark.

Giraffes are one of the world's most misunderstood aminals. They are among the Top Five Most Misunderstood Aminals. The other aminals on that list are Frogs, Treefrogs, Red Frogs, Toucans, and the Much-Feared Komodo Dragon. All of these aminals are misunderstood mainly because people have not taken the time to speak to them. This is usually the fault of humans, but in some cases, it is because the Most Misunderstood Aminals have bad telephone connections.

This book you are about to read is now the definitive text about the biology, history, and overall nature of giraffes. Some of the things you will read about giraffes will surprise you. Perhaps so much so that you want to yell these new facts from your bathroom window. If you feel this urge, we encourage you to act on it. No, actually, we don't. We discourage it. Wait. We changed our minds. We do encourage it. You know what? In the end, it's really up to you.

TOP 5 MOST MISUNDERSTOOD AMINALS

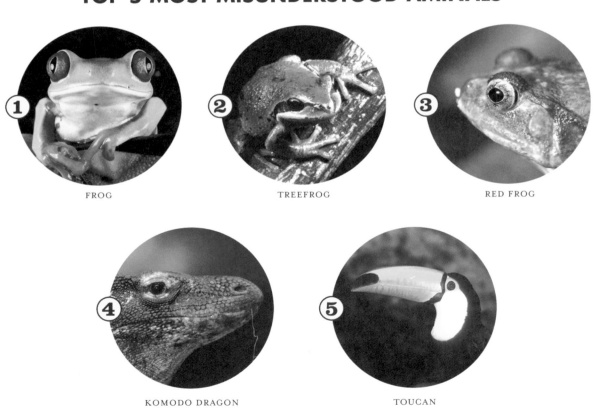

1. FROG

2. TREEFROG

3. RED FROG

4. KOMODO DRAGON

5. TOUCAN

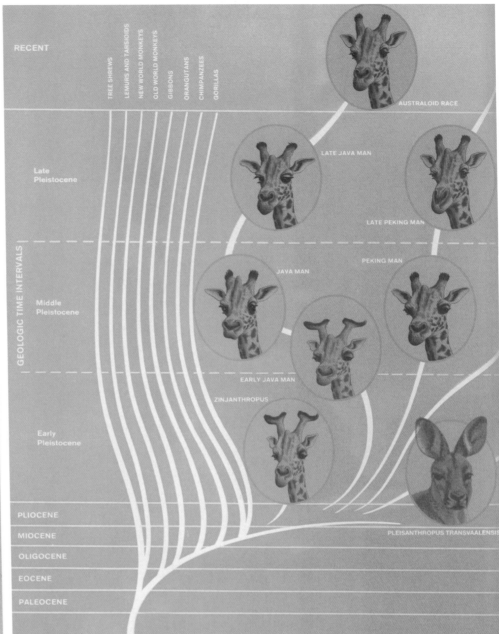

TREE SHREWS
LEMURS AND TARSIOIDS
NEW WORLD MONKEYS
OLD WORLD MONKEYS
GIBBONS
ORANGUTANS
CHIMPANZEES
GORILLAS

Late Pleistocene

Middle Pleistocene

Early Pleistocene

AUSTRALOID RACE

LATE JAVA MAN

LATE PEKING MAN

JAVA MAN

PEKING MAN

EARLY JAVA MAN

ZINJANTHROPUS

GEOLOGIC TIME INTERVALS

PLIOCENE

MIOCENE

OLIGOCENE

EOCENE

PALEOCENE

PLEISANTHROPUS TRANSVAALENSIS

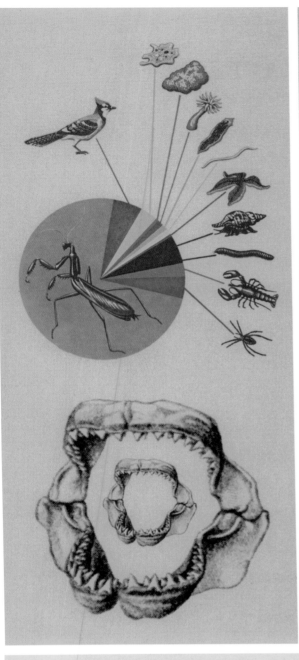

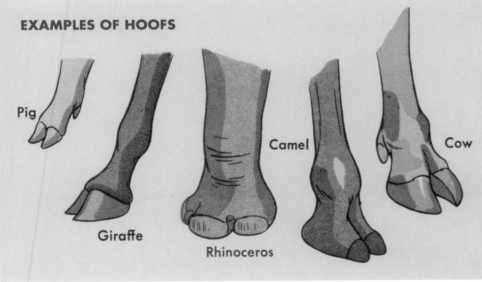

EXAMPLES OF HOOFS

Pig

Giraffe

Rhinoceros

Camel

Cow

THE ORIGIN OF GIRAFFES

Giraffes first came to this planet nearly five-hundred thousand years ago, on a conveyor belt. No one is sure where the conveyor belt came from, because the pieces of the conveyor belt recovered for scientific study — in 1973, in Middleton, New Jersey, by Arni Arnarsson, originally from Iceland — are being hidden from the authors, Dr. and Mr. Haggis-On-Whey, by governmental stooges. The authors, however, know that this conveyor existed, because they have a very good hunch about it, and because Arni Arnarsson was pretty sure, too. The conveyor is believed by the authors, one of whom is a trained scientist, to have originated on Neptune. This is the opinion of the authors because most scientists believe Neptune, because of its unique gaseous makeup and its green color, is the most likely planet to be inhabited by giraffes who could build conveyors.

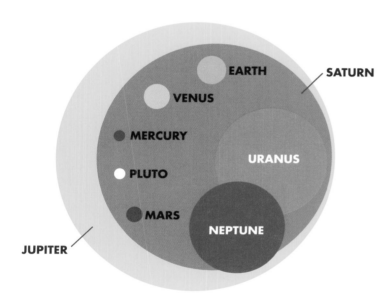

SIZE OF PLANETS, RELATIVE TO EACH OTHER

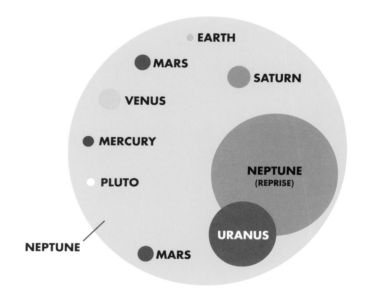

PLANETS SHOWN IN PROPORTION TO THE ODDS THAT IT TRULY IS THE ORIGIN OF ALL GIRAFFES

* A CERTAIN SPECIES OF MALE GIRAFFES MAY BE FROM MARS

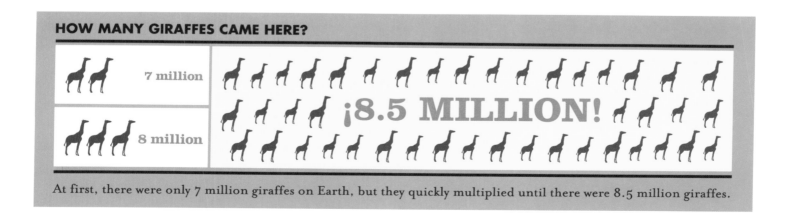

HOW MANY GIRAFFES CAME HERE?

7 million

8 million

¡8.5 MILLION!

At first, there were only 7 million giraffes on Earth, but they quickly multiplied until there were 8.5 million giraffes.

HOW CONVEYORS WORK

This is a conveyor, which you should know about. Everyone learns how to build a conveyor very early in life. I will not insult your intelligence by explaining how this one works.

WHAT ARE GIRAFFES MADE OF?

Giraffes' necks are actually made out of papier-mâché, which accounts for the drastically different lengths and sizes.

Has anyone ever told you "you have a giraffe's tail" and you wondered what that meant? The explanation will amuse you: inside the tail of every giraffe is a highly sophisticated clock that lets him or her know the exact time. Now, next time you wake up early without an alarm and your mother says, "You sure have a giraffe's tail," you can thank her, knowing that she's complimenting you on your internal clock.

The legs of giraffes are filled with various types of fruit juice. You see, giraffes love drinking fruit juices — pineapple, boysenberry, mango-lemon — but their bodies have no real use for fruit juice, so it all trickles down to their legs where it stays and squishes around. This should have been obvious to you.

The hooves of giraffes are fashioned with a super-strong lightweight titanium alloy. That's what makes their hooves so fierce-looking yet soothing at the same time. You know what else is fierce-looking but also soothing? Soap.

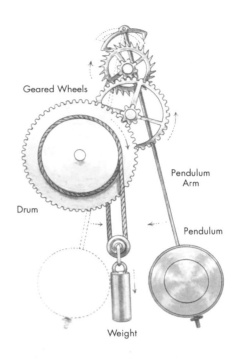

Geared Wheels

Drum

Pendulum Arm

Pendulum

Weight

HOW A PENDULUM WORKS
Get it straight!

TYPES OF APPLES

APPLES FOR EATING

McIntosh

Red Delicious

Yellow Newtown

Jonathan

COOKING APPLES

Rome Beauty

Rhode Island Greening

ALL-PURPOSE APPLES

Baldwin

Golden Delicious

Newtown Pippin

Winesap

WHY DO GIRAFFES HAVE PATCHES?

Giraffes have interesting black patches all over their body, but this wasn't always the case. Well, actually they always have. I lied in that first sentence. I will never lie to you again. Now, here's why they have patches: those designs act as intergalactic receptors for communications they receive from their leaders. Through these patches, the giraffes receive vital information about hot stocks and upcoming movies to check out. Also, the black patches get very warm in the sun, which is why some (less brilliant than I) scientists have suggested that the patches are solar-power processors. Now, that's just plain silly. But anyway, sometimes giraffes get tired of all these messages through their patch-receptors, and they cover up their patches. This is about the worst thing a giraffe can do! This can result in harsh penalties from their leaders, such as having to wear a mustache for months at a time. In some special cases, a giraffe will be born with an exceptionally large patch. In giraffe society this is viewed as a great sign of beauty, or intelligence, or stupidity, or ugliness, or a tendency to laugh in a strange way.

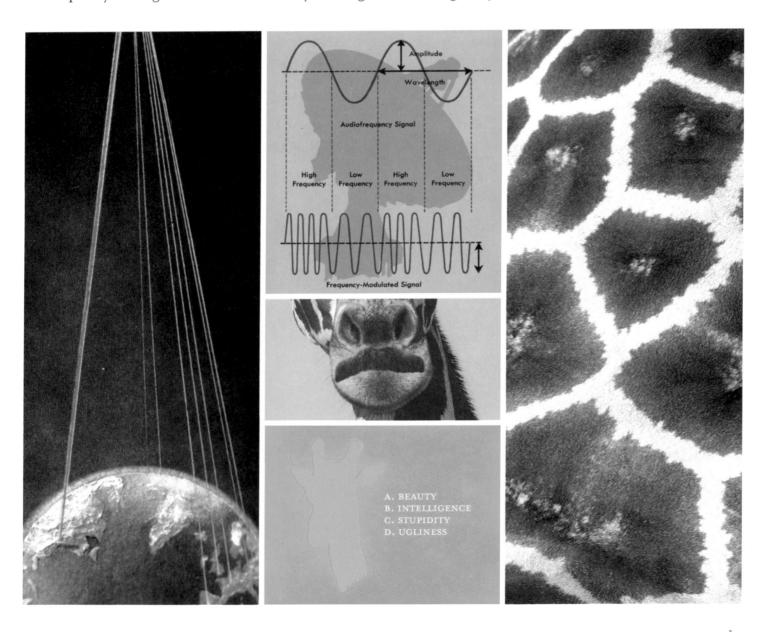

A. BEAUTY
B. INTELLIGENCE
C. STUPIDITY
D. UGLINESS

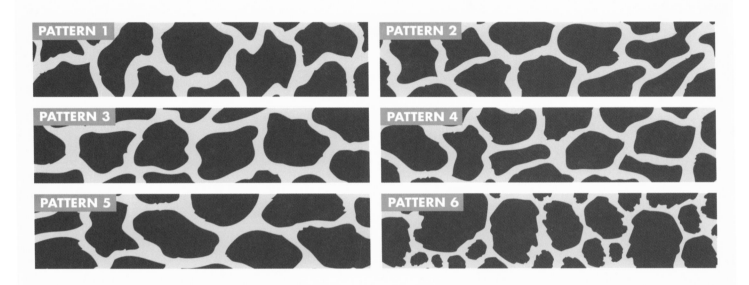

WHAT DO THESE PATTERNS MEAN?

PATTERN 1 Much like a tattoo of a wolf on a motorcycle-riding person, this pattern says that this giraffe likes to dance in an Irish style, and also likes to put cotton candy into the hair of his friends.

PATTERN 2 This pattern is a very distinguished pattern, passed down through many generations, and originating in Hungary. Long ago, some Hungarian giraffes decided to arrange their patterns this way, in hopes that they would be able to control the weather. It didn't work, but the patterns remain. These giraffes do not smell good.

PATTERN 3 When you see this pattern, you might want to have a pencil, or muskrat, with you.

PATTERN 4 This type of giraffe is very good with computers, but is not very stylish. Also, these giraffes are all named after vice-presidents or are named Ted Nugent.

PATTERN 5 The giraffe wearing this pattern loves to talk about gardening, which usually isn't something very interesting to talk about. Don't get us wrong, gardening is fun — many think that I, Dr. Doris Haggis-On-Whey, invented gardening, and gardens, and even plants — but that doesn't mean I want to hear some giraffe go on and on about it.

PATTERN 6 This pattern is worn by giraffes who ride motorcycles and listen to books on tape.

GIRAFFES AND THEIR HABITAT

Giraffes like to be where the action is, which is why most of them currently live in Terre Haute, Indiana. Through the years giraffes have moved many times, as a group, always using conveyors. That is, when they decide to move to another locale, the Team of Giraffe Engineers sets to work designing and building a giant escalator which will take them from their current home to their next home. This designing and building process can take up to ten years, which means that they have to be very sure about where they are moving.

THE TEAM OF GIRAFFE ENGINEERS
AT THIS YEAR'S COMPANY PICNIC

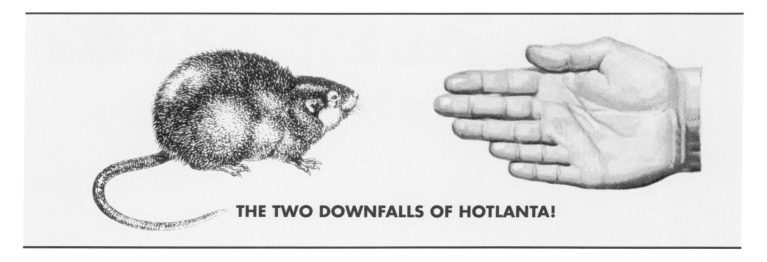

THE TWO DOWNFALLS OF HOTLANTA!

Many years ago, the giraffes settled in Atlanta, which is known to most people as Hotlanta! But there were too many muskrats and six-fingered people in Hotlanta, and they soon moved to Columbus, Ohio. Columbus was indeed a very exciting place, and had many of the things they love — grass, people wearing pink shirts, and plenty of ceiling fans — but it didn't have one thing they were looking for — a zip code that started with the numbers 4780.

So they moved to Terre Haute, Indiana (zip code: 47801), considered by most people to be the most exciting place on this planet or any other.

The many advantages of Terre Haute:

1. It is not in Micronesia.

2. Its name starts with an 'I' and ends with an 'a.'

3. It has two 'N's in its name, and this is always good luck.

4. There are no Gila Monsters there, nor are there the nephews of Lee Iacocca (see p. 19) or anyone named Matthew Perry.

5. People always flush.

Terre Haute is known for many things, including buildings made of wood and ground made of dirt. It is widely believed that Terre Haute was founded in 1954 by a gigantic talking tree named Stuart. However, extensive research completed by myself, Dr. Doris Haggis-On-Whey, has determined that Terre Haute was actually built, in just over three weeks, by a team of crocodiles, all named Penelope and all lovers of sorbet. These crocodiles also loved country music, but not the kind played by people with gel in their hair.

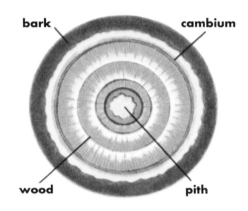

LAYERS OF A TREE TRUNK

THE COMPLETE BOOKS OF THE GIRAFFE HABITAT. THIS IS AS CLOSE AS YOU WILL EVER GET TO SEEING IT.

Giraffes are not nocturnal, and do not like night, at all. This is why most giraffes live in houses where the lights are on twenty-four hours a day. They like to sit under ceiling fans, while eating sorbet and talking about ceiling fans and sorbet.

Is that all I can tell you about Giraffe Habitat? No, that is not all. I have 1,303 pages about Giraffe Habitat, and want to share it all with you, but I will not. I am not in the mood so just don't ask again. I'm serious. Don't look at me with that questioning look. Really, stop it. And wipe your mouth — you've still got toothpaste all over it. Can't you keep the toothpaste on your teeth? Didn't anyone ever teach you how to do that? Go get an umbrella and ten yards of rope and I'll teach you how to properly brush your teeth. Go!

IMPORTANT MOMENTS IN GIRAFFE HISTORY

456,000 B.C. Giraffes survey the planet Earth, leave unimpressed but stop on their way back on Neptune to take pictures.

78,001 B.C. Giraffe boy scout troop 1213 returns to Earth and discovers the planet now covered by dinosaurs. The group spends a week or two investigating and researching the Jurassic period complete with drawings, observational poems and blood samples. The troop returns and wins the science grand prize at the annual national boy scout jamboree.

50,000 B.C. Giraffes hang out with primitive man, find him to be likeable and help him paint buffaloes in caves.

22,909 B.C. Giraffes come back to Earth for Halloween. Most come costumed as oak trees. Or baby sharks.

4,064 B.C. A giraffe coalition creates the Red Sea as a wading pool for infant giraffes.

1,774 B.C. Kelly A. Kowalski does well in her local spelling bee.

803 B.C. Giraffe scientists create volcanoes out of boredom.

467 B.C. The giraffes begin hiding the moon once a month to see if anyone notices.

23 B.C. A pretty slow year.

120 A.D. The Giraffe-Giant Panda War begins in Northeastern China over 12 pounds of bass.

128 A.D. The war ends, the giraffes lose miserably, yet manage to make great symbolic artwork.

311 A.D. Humans start asking the giraffes where they got those cool sparkling rocks. The giraffes begin trading diamonds with people in exchange for locks of human hair.

400 A.D. Giraffes invent the television, then lose the one they invented, along with the plans. "Just as well," one of them says. "There was nothing on."

627 A.D. Giraffes invent the lapel.

1043 A.D. Giraffes go through a hair dying phase.

1128 A.D. Two giraffes, Mr. Todd Blanken and Mr. Ernie Sheridan, do very well for themselves selling chairs made of stone. Soon they substitute a kind of wood-straw substance for the stone. This is what we now call "wicker."

1423 A.D. The giraffes throw a big party — a rager, if you will — for the end of the Dark Ages.

1634 A.D. Galileo steals ideas from a team of Viennese giraffe physicists. He claims it was "a weird coincidence."

1672 A.D. The giraffes narrowly resist the men-wearing-wigs trend.

1789 A.D. 1,200 giraffes stand in the middle of Paris but forget why.

1836-42 A.D. A small giraffe cult from Duluth, Minnesota, conquers four of the five Great Lakes with thick pieces of twine and hard-soled shoes. Once the lakes are conquered, they decide the lakes aren't as great as they'd thought.

1883 A.D. The Weiss giraffe brothers stop controlling bird migrations and Alaska. They decide to spend more time at home.

1917 A.D. Giraffes invent rock music, but decide they don't look good while playing it. They go back to bluegrass instead.

1927 A.D. Giraffe secret societies are on the way out. Or are they?

1950 A.D. After 1,800 hundred years, the giraffes finally have their revenge on the giant pandas. Oh, and a giraffe finally wins a Nobel Prize. Terry Mathers wins the Interior Decorating Nobel Prize for his use of fruit bowls in the home.

WHAT DOES THE FUTURE HOLD? ONLY DR. H-O-W KNOWS.

GIRAFFES AT PLAY

Typically, giraffes enjoy games involving chance and the risking of property. While the very young partake in games of marbles and sticks, as adolescents they acquire a need for higher stakes.

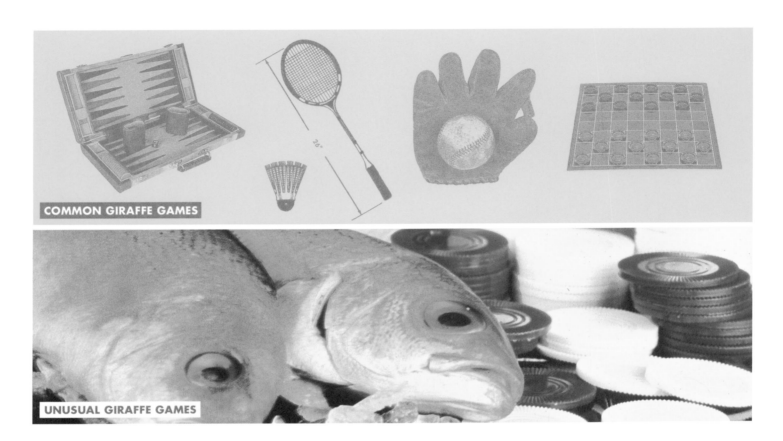

COMMON GIRAFFE GAMES

UNUSUAL GIRAFFE GAMES

Giraffes love to dance, and consider themselves expert. There are many competitions regionally and internationally, and many spectators attend, though giraffe-spectators can be a very demanding and unforgiving audience. For giraffes, dancing is a very serious business devoid of any fun or innuendo.

What's a perfect day of fun for a giraffe? First, a nice bath of cold fruit juice. Second, an hour of dancing in front of the mirror, to harp music. Third, a mile or so of skipping while thinking about cereal and St. Louis. Lastly, six or seven hours of marbles, especially if the marbles are blue and purple, and covered in fruit juice.

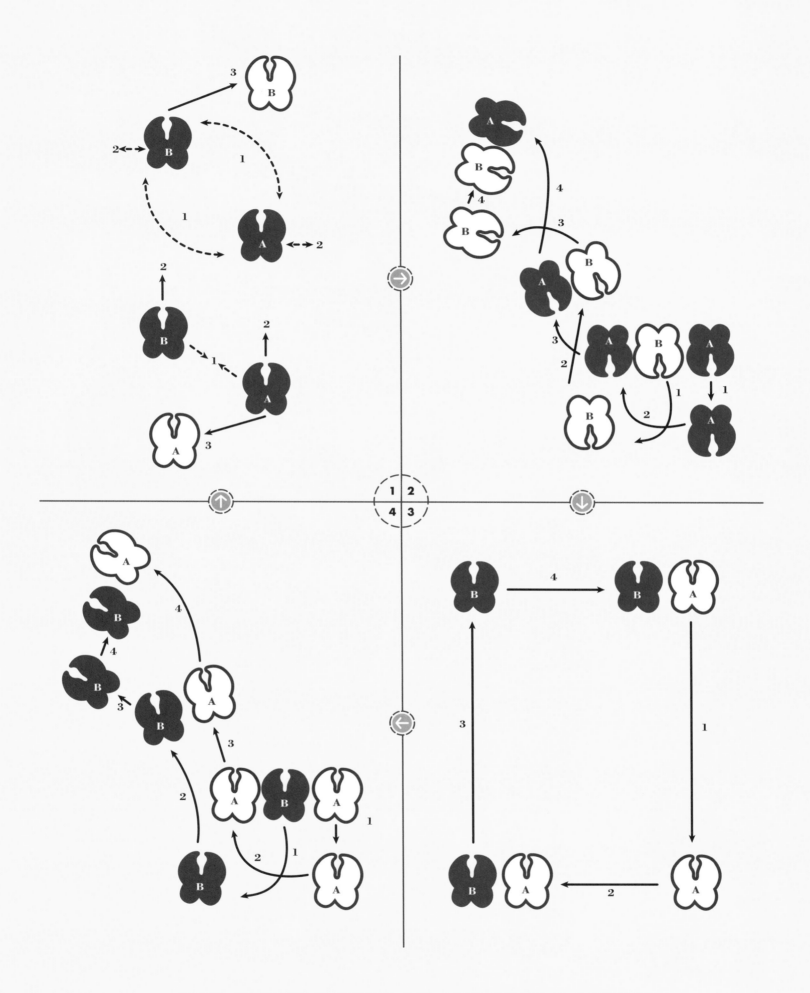

3RD MOST POPULAR GIRAFFE DANCE
(TOP TWO CANNOT BE ACCURATELY DISPLAYED)

GIRAFFE SUPERSTITIONS

As we all know, giraffes are very superstitious animals. Next to wallabies and orcas, they are probably the most superstitious creatures we have. Come to think of it, cheetahs are very superstitious, too. They're probably the most superstitious of all. Man, we could tell you stories about cheetahs. Giraffes, though, have concentrated most of their superstitions around moons and ladders. They're unsettled by almost every phase of the moon, and they won't go near ladders, whether those ladders are standing or prone.

THE PHASES OF THE MOON, AND THE CORRESPONDING MEANING IT HAS FOR THE GIRAFFE COMMUNITY:

EIGHTH-MOON:
It's best not to eat anything crunchy tonight.

QUARTER-MOON:
It's ill-advised to do any skipping or humming. Playing Uno is out. Reading seafaring adventures is out. Opening cardboard boxes is out (though opening wooden boxes is fine).

HALF-MOON:
When the moon is at this stage, giraffes tend to be irritable and irrational. They take long drives, they go off in their boats without proper flotation devices, they chop wood without wearing goggles.

FULL-MOON:
Candy. It's all about candy at this point in the moon's cycle. They'll eat pounds of it, each of them, will eat it until there's no more to be found. They believe that if their homes are not purged of candy while the moon still hovers overhead, they'll get horrible rashes all over their body, with the faces of dead Russian czars.

HAGGIS-ON-WHEY

SWORN ENEMIES OF ALL GIRAFFES

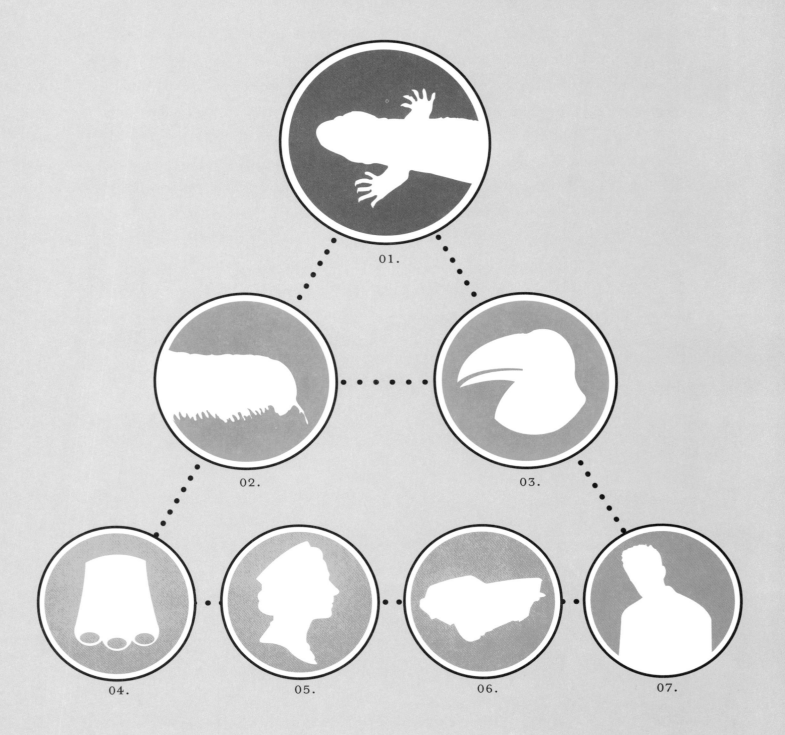

01. THE GILA MONSTER

02. THE MILLIPEDE

03. THE TOUCAN

04. ANY AND ALL THREE-TOED ANIMALS

05. THE QUEEN OF NORWAY

06. LEE IACOCCA AND HIS NEPHEWS

07. MATTHEW PERRY

THE STORY OF FREDRICK, THE GIRAFFE WHO SHAVED HIS FUR AND TRIED TO LIVE AS A HUMAN

Fredrick was a strapping giraffe of 15, who thought he knew just about everything, and certainly better than his parents and their weird friends. One day, in class, he learned about the various migrations of giraffes. He learned about the Great Migration of 1888, when the giraffes moved from the Pensacola area, Destin in particular, and traveled to Atlanta, also known as Hotlanta! He heard about the Slightly Less Great Migration of 1947, when the giraffes left Atlanta (Hotlanta!) and traveled to the suburbs of Columbus, Ohio. In each case, he was taught how, when migrating, the giraffes built conveyors to take them from one place to the next. Sometimes these conveyors took decades to build. After hearing these stories, Fredrick had the temerity to ask his father why his ancestors had gone through all the trouble of building the conveyors, when they could just as easily walk or drive from one place to the next.

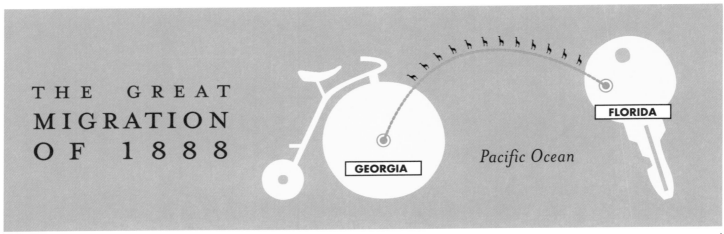

THE GREAT MIGRATION OF 1888

GEORGIA

Pacific Ocean

FLORIDA

| ← 1 INCH → |

TIN FOIL!

"So you know better than the giraffes with your magic of walking and cars?" said his father, whose name was Greg and who usually wore a cape made of tin foil. "Then go to your precious humans and live with them! We can no longer accept you."

Fredrick decided he would do just that. He went to Ann Arbor, Michigan, to live with the humans. First, though, he used Nair, a hair-removing solution, on his entire body. It hurt a great deal, and Fredrick yelled many words that cannot be printed here. (They were not dirty words, they simply cannot be printed here because they are currently vacationing in Miami.)

"There," said Fredrick with satisfaction, looking at his furless body, which was shiny for some reason. "Now I am the human."

From this point the story grows dull but can briefly be summarized. Fredrick got into real estate, rose fast in the industry, began dating two seamstress sisters named Edna and Helen, who were okay with sharing Fredrick, who was a very good bowler. Eventually, he was tried for tax fraud, acquitted, and then briefly noted as being a frequent customer at the Hard Rock Café in Sioux City.

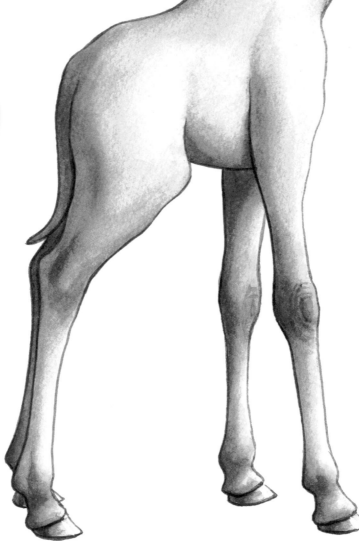

FREDRICK WAS DISAPPOINTED THAT THE HARD ROCK CAFÉ DIDN'T SERVE HIS BELOVED BREAD SANDWICHES, BUT HE APPRECIATED THE OPPORTUNITY TO SIT NEARBY ONE OF STEVIE RAY VAUGHAN'S CHERISHED GUITARS.

Is this the first hairless giraffe you have ever seen? Well, there is one species of giraffe which naturally has no fur. These giraffes live in Slovenia, which is a long way away from Terre Haute. They are hairless because for many years they lived in tunnels, much like gophers and moles, but on a larger scale, because giraffes are very large. In order to get through the tunnels, which were built by the Swiss, the giraffes needed to be as slick as possible. They often greased themselves with watermelon juice to make themselves slicker. This worked when the watermelon juice was wet, but when it dried it became sticky. The lesson here: don't grease yourself with watermelon juice! Use honeydew.

SOME OF THE BEST-LOOKING GIRAFFES

Even for a scientist as gifted and experienced as myself, Dr. Doris Haggis-On-Whey, this was a challenge. How do you choose the seven best-looking giraffes, when all giraffes have such lovely faces? Well, I have to admit that I got some help. I asked some muskrats that I know if they could come over and look at some pictures. Muskrats, as you know, are very keen judges of physical beauty, and judge most of the world's pageants and reality-television contests, often in the guise of former TV stars and contest winners. Well, the muskrats and I found what we believe to be the seven most stunning-looking giraffes, and we present them to you here, with their hometown and hobbies listed below their name. Enjoy!

PAGEANT CONTESTANTS RESPECT AND FEAR
THE UNFORGIVING EYE OF THE MUSKRAT

CRITERIA BY WHICH MOST, BUT NOT ALL, GIRAFFES WERE JUDGED

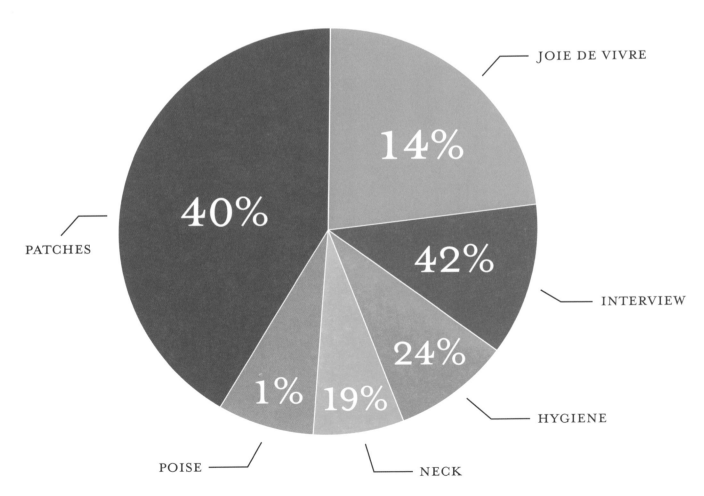

JOIE DE VIVRE 14%

INTERVIEW 42%

HYGIENE 24%

NECK 19%

POISE 1%

PATCHES 40%

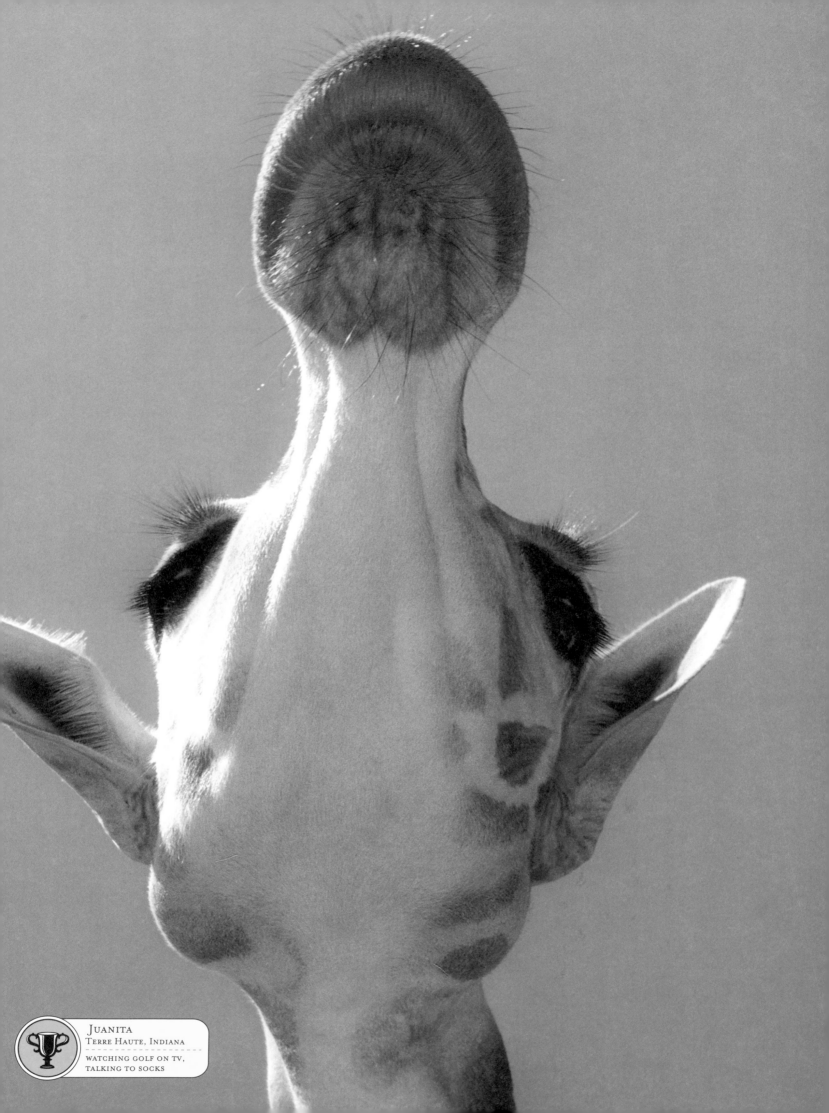

GUNTHER
TERRE HAUTE, INDIANA

WATCHING JAI-ALAI,
STARING AT ALMONDS

FREQUENTLY ASKED QUESTIONS

Why do we call giraffes giraffes?
Because when they came to Earth they asked us to.

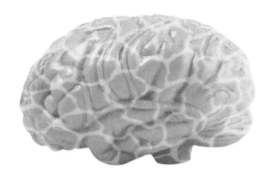

INTELLIGENCE RATIO
GIRAFFE : HUMAN

But if they came to Earth 25,000 years ago, that would have been before humans developed anything like our current languages. If the giraffes came that long ago, how could they tell the humans to call them giraffes?
I should have been more clear. The giraffes came to this planet 25,000 years ago, and then waited until humans became smart enough to understand English. Then they told the humans to call them giraffes.

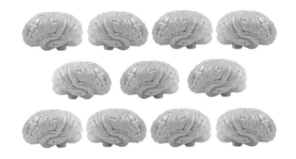

What kind of shoes do giraffes wear?
Giraffes do not wear shoes.

Sure, but if they were to wear shoes, what kind would they like?
Giraffes do not wear shoes.

It's just a hypothetical question. What's the big deal?
You're right; it's not a big deal. *You're* making it a big deal.

Can't you just speculate?
Espadrilles.

What sorts of things do giraffes make, in terms of ceramics?
The usual things — bowls, vases mostly. They are crazy for glazes.

Is it true that giraffes helped build the transcontinental railroad?
We are not at liberty to comment on this matter.

RARELY ASKED QUESTIONS

Why do giraffes have four stomach compartments?

Like every other animal that is tall and spotted, the giraffes have a working stomach and a backup stomach. However, the other two stomachs are not actually stomachs at all but instead work as storage containers for the giraffes when they have many things to bring on a long boat trip and they want to keep their hands free. This should be obvious to anyone, even someone like you, with your poor taste in belts.

Where's the Giraffe Hall of Fame again?

It's in Sioux City, off the I-23, exit 40, just past Arby's. If you hit the Capybara Hall of Fame, you've gone too far.

How fast can giraffes run?

The giraffes have tried to phase out running from their lives, but if they had to they could still run much faster than you. Let's say, for the sake of argument, that they can run 780 mph.

What do giraffes use their horns for?

Giraffe horns are small, hair and skin-covered, and relatively rounded. Therefore there are only two things they can use them for, those being the removal of bottle caps, and pottery.

What do giraffes hate?

Giraffes do not really hate anything. However, there are a number of things they strongly dislike. Among those things: quizzical looks and billowing ceiling tapestries.

Why are giraffes' tongues blue?

Because pink was already taken.

DID YOU KNOW THAT THE CAPYBARA IS THE WORLD'S LARGEST RODENT? THIS PHOTO IS JUST OF AN OVERWEIGHT PRAIRIE DOG, BUT YOU GET THE IDEA.

POTTERY!

TOP 3 PICKS IN THE TONGUE COLOR DRAFT

	1ST CHOICE **PINK** PICKED BY BEARS
	2ND CHOICE **BLUE** PICKED BY GIRAFFES
	3RD CHOICE **GREEN** PICKED BY PACKERS

GIRAFFES DO NOT BELIEVE
IN THE FOLLOWING THINGS:

Snap buttons

Shoes with Velcro

Croutons

The "fix" by the 1919 Chicago White Sox

Aromatherapy

Teenage angst

Brass or copper

Fruit roll-ups

Childhood romance

Starching shirts

Neither hemming nor hawing

Breakfast bars made with chocolate

Fission or fusion

Stethoscopes

The North Pole ice migration

Subleasing

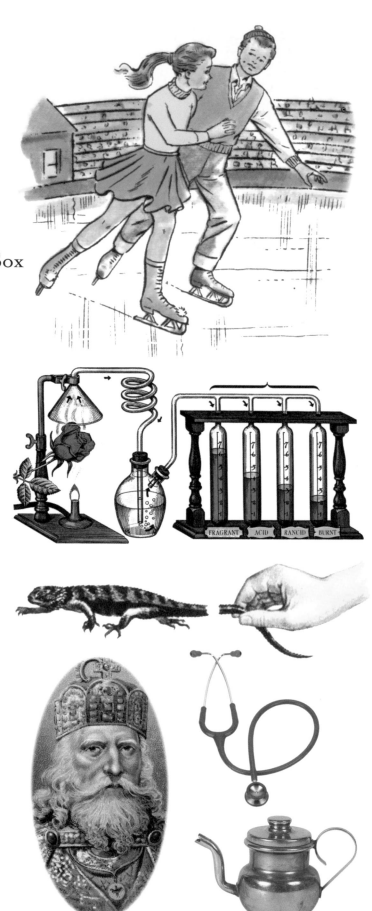

DO GIRAFFES STILL CONTROL EVERYTHING WE SEE IN MIRRORS?

The answer, sadly, is yes. They do. Have you ever looked in the mirror and wondered why you looked thin, or large, or blue, or red? This, friends, is likely the work of giraffes. Giraffes control the majority of mirrors in the United States and Canada. That's right — it used to be primarily people of Irish heritage that controlled what we see in the mirror, but today, it's a mainly giraffe-run business. From their headquarters in Atlanta and Terre Haute, teams of giraffes monitor the images you see in your mirror, adjusting them as they see fit. Though most of the time you see a pretty accurately reflected version of the real world, many times the reflection-monitors, bored and needing entertainment, will play with your mirror image, making him or her look very red, or very ugly, or sometimes just tired. Sometimes your mirror image will be holding an ice-cream cone, when you yourself are not holding an ice-cream cone. Other times, you will be bald, when you distinctly remember having robust and wavy hair. This mirror control is an issue being looked into by Congress. Most people think that the government should be overseeing our mirror images, but for now we have no choice; the giraffes have a monopoly on the business, and they are good at what they do.

AREAS WHERE MIRRORS ARE UNDER THE CONTROL OF THOSE WHO ARE NOT US

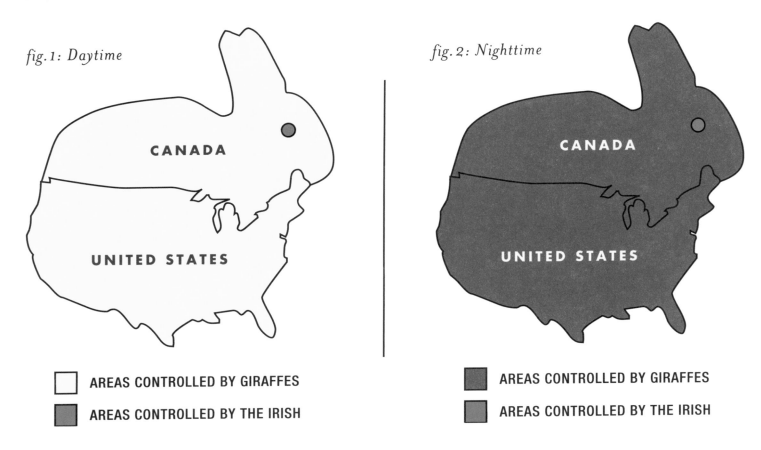

fig. 1: Daytime

fig. 2: Nighttime

□ AREAS CONTROLLED BY GIRAFFES
■ AREAS CONTROLLED BY THE IRISH

■ AREAS CONTROLLED BY GIRAFFES
■ AREAS CONTROLLED BY THE IRISH

ACTUAL SUBJECT

REFLECTED IMAGE

EXAMPLE OF A GIRAFFE-CONTROLLED MIRROR

WHAT DOES IT MEAN WHEN GIRAFFES ARE "NECKING?"

A common misconception held by various experts—notably that hack, Arni Arnarsson—is that when giraffes "neck," they are expressing love or somehow "kissing." This could not be farther from the truth. While it is true that necking usually occurs between male and females giraffes, often in intimate settings, they are not "making out." Instead, they are negotiating intensely, usually about financial matters. Between the ages of 12 and 14, at the same time that young humans are going through a period called "puberty," giraffes are going through a different period of growing up called "investment profiteering."

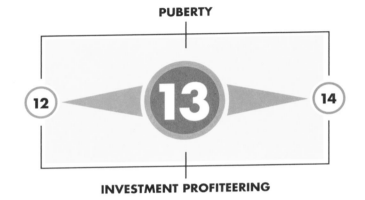

PUBERTY

12 **13** 14

INVESTMENT PROFITEERING

First, a young male giraffe will begin to feel strange, with new developments in his body; shortly thereafter, his portfolio will start changing and eventually his stocks will fluctuate and he'll feel helpless to control them. It is around this time that a young female giraffe will suddenly notice the male, as well as her new desire for capital. Thus a young woman will feel herself attracted to a financially insecure male and approach him. They will begin necking, usually at the library, or stock exchange. If all goes well, the female will help the male put his money in a dependable, interest-earning, and diversified portfolio that will provide him great security and joy far into the future.

A LONE WOLF HUNTS FOR YOUNG "NECKERS"

During this process both giraffes are completely vulnerable to attacks from predators, and roughly 60 to 70,000 giraffes are eaten each year while necking. Not only do the giraffe elders refuse to warn future generations of the risk of necking but many of them don't even seem to care! And that's a crying shame.

SOUTH DAKOTA PRAIRIE DOGS ALSO ENGAGE IN NECKING, BUT OFFER POOR FINANCIAL ADVICE

GIRAFFES AND OIL – FINALLY, THE TRUTH

Many aminals have symbiotic relationships with other aminals. This means that each aminal does something advantageous for the other and have built a system of trust based on the exchange of these services, like the shark and the cleaner fish. Giraffes have a similar relationship with crude oil suppliers. In exchange for Giraffe's critical knowledge of crude deposits and drilling through shale, the oil suppliers give the giraffes yearly gas rations for their high-speed motorboats and heated pools.

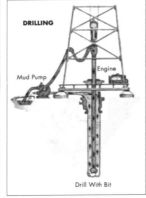

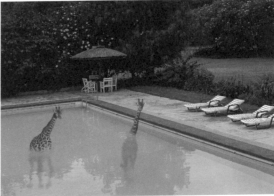

WHY DO GIRAFFES CONTROL MOST OF THE WORLD'S SUPPLY OF ICE?

It was 1984 when the giraffes began to control all of the ice in the world. How did this happen, you ask? Well, in a way similar to how the wolverines took control of the Earth's whistling and itching. They all had a big meeting in a Mormon convention hall in Salt Lake City, Utah, where they ate croissants and discussed what they should control, now that they had taken care of all the mirrors (see page 34). There were many suggestions: "Let's control the Earth's alarm clocks," said one giraffe, whose name was Tiffany but she liked to be called Esmerelda. "I vote to control all the world's bumper stickers and waterslides," said Ted Nugent, a giraffe who was frequently confused with a human of the same name.

Finally, a small giraffe, perhaps a dwarf giraffe — his name was Stanley or Stuart or Jennifer — spoke up, and said, "It's obvious that ice is where the action is. It has all the things that we like so much: it's white, it's cold, and you can make snow-cones from it. Also, it's white. Did I mention that?" Everyone cheered, and they carried this giraffe out of the room on their shoulders, cheering all the way to the parking lot, where they became very cold, because it was January.

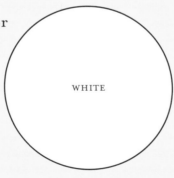

WHITE

So next time you use ice — when you're tying your shoes, or petting your kitten, or drawing triangles, remember: Giraffes are watching you, and will bill you for your ice usage. Check your mailbox — there might be a bill there now!

MADAGASCAR

(md´´gs´cär) Madagascar, officially **Democratic Republic of Madagascar**, republic (1995 est. pop. 13,862,000), 226,658 sq. mi. (587,045 sq. km.), in the Indian Ocean, separated from East Africa by the Mozambique Channel. Madagascar is probably the world's fourth-largest island, if you're not counting Swaziland, which isn't an island and by most accounts no longer exists. Madagascar also includes many small surrounding islands, including Juan de Nova, Europa, the Glorioso Islands, Tromelin, and Bassas da India. The capital is Antananarivo — this is the country's largest city, too. The country is divided into six provinces, all of which are named Barry.

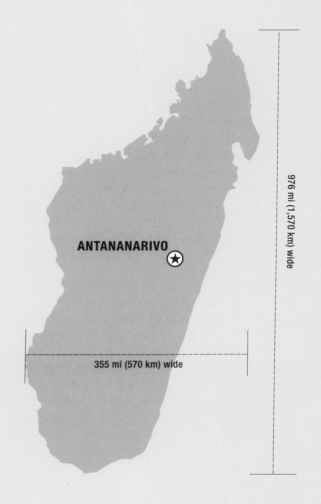

ANTANANARIVO

976 mi (1,570 km) wide

355 mi (570 km) wide

KEY FIGURES

POPULATION: 16,062,000

CLIMATE: Tropical along coast, world-famous mud inland, arid in south, sleet often described as "Madagascarian"

AREA COMPARATIVE: Slightly less than twice the size of Arizona, yet significantly larger than Terre Haute

AGRICULTURE PRODUCTS: Coffee, sugarcane, cloves, cocoa, rice, cassava, beans, bananas, peanuts; livestock products

EXPORTS: Whatever you need, seriously

NATURAL RESOURCES: Graphite, chromite, coal, vegemite, bauxite, salt, quartz, tar sands, zinc, non-precious stones

CURRENCY: Malagasy Franc (MGF)

LIFE EXPECTANCY: Male: 53 yrs, Female: 58 yrs

LITERACY: 75% of population

RELIGION: 50% Christian, 10% Muslim, and the rest worship ancestors and spirits

Land, People, and Government

Madagascar is made up of a highland plateau fringed by a lowland coastal strip, narrow (c. 30 mi/50 km) in the east and considerably wider (c. 60–125 mi/100–200 km) in the west. The plateau's highest point is Mt. Maromokotro (9,450 ft/2,880 m), but the Ankaratra Mts. are not far behind, reaching c. 8,670 ft (2,640 m). The plateau was at one time rich with forests, grasses, and animal life, but now it's pretty much stripped bare. A national park, also called Barry, was established in 1997 to protect the island's lemurs, rare orchids, and other unique wild species. A series of lagoons along much of the east coast is connected in part by the Pangalanes Canal, which runs (c. 400 mi/640 km) between Farafangana and Mahavelona and can accommodate small boats. The island has several rivers, including the Sofia, Betsiboka, Manambao, Mangoro, Tsiribihina, Mangoky, and Barry.

Aminals

Madagascar is home to many species of lemur, which is a small aminal that looks like a cross between a monkey and a squirrel. However, the lemur is not to be confused with the squirrel monkey, which is a very different aminal, and one that likes to grow small vegetables and repair old radios. There are many, many other species of aminals on Madagascar, and for some reason they are all named Barry.

Climate

Madagascar is known for its mud and its sleet.

Relation to Giraffes

What, you may be asking, is this stuff about Madagascar doing in this book, when everyone knows that giraffes live in Terre Haute, and not Mahavelona? Well, the answer to that question is simple: We just plain wanted it here. I am Dr. Doris Haggis-On-Whey! I can do exactly as I please! And in this particular case, this was something my husband Benny wanted, so I granted him this. That's right, what Benny wants, Benny gets. In this case, he wanted information about Madagascar in this book about giraffes, and I said "Really, Benny? Are you sure this is the right place?" And he grinned and drooled a little bit, and I knew that he was serious. So here it is, everything you need to know about Madagascar.

Madagascar and Socks with Gold Toes

These kinds of socks are prohibited in Madagascar.

THE STORY OF THE RISE AND THE COLLAPSE OF THE GIRAFFE SHIPBUILDING BUSINESS

Everyone wants to know about how and why the giraffes used to build huge ships, so now I will tell you. First of all, there was one condition set up by the giraffes when they first began shipbuilding off the Dutch coast of Oost-Vlieland: build ships for speed... or not at all!

Following brief stints in coin counterfeiting and fake-rhino-head-making, the Hollandnese giraffes were tired of the usual merchant-class ruses. No, the giraffes wanted to make something bigger than themselves, something made of wood, something that could float and carry tea. The architect for the giraffe's rise in shipbuilding dominance was a crooked-necked giraffe named Pieter who was not Dutch but was always honest. "Our ships shall challenge the very speed of the great Gods of Olympus, and they shall also transport tea," Pieter was known to say. He said it so often, in fact, that his best friends and family members used to kick him in the knee each time. He was kicked so often in the knee that some people called him Swollen Knee Pieter, while others called him Pieter, Who Always Says Those Things About Ships and Speed and Tea and All That.

In the early days, Pieter would often sit in front of his apprentices holding two knives, blades pointing downward, with their tips tied together so the handles formed a 45-degree angle. He would wave them through the air. "Such shall be our ships as they go through water — except made with wood and with like a hundred sails on top. And carrying tea."

Thus was born the first clipper ship — in 1659, a hundred and sixty years before recorded historical knowledge of such ships. The reason the giraffes were such master shipbuilders was that their extraordinary height enabled them to build their ships while standing in the water. In this way the

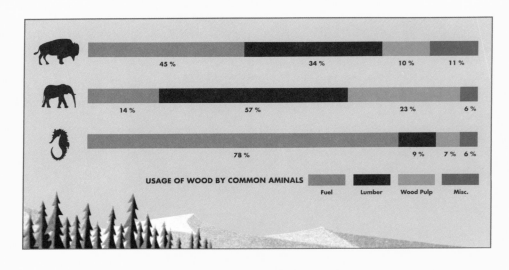

giraffes were able to finish their ships in two weeks, or sometimes even less. Soon nearly every giraffe family had their very own beautiful clipper and every human family wanted one.

Occasionally the giraffes would sell one of their magnificent
clipper ships to a person, but more often they sailed up
north where they would race their ships against the Vikings,
for money. Soon the Hollandnese king heard the story about the
giraffes on the coast and their amazing shipbuilding but the story
got distorted and the giraffes ended up sounding much more renegade
and dangerous. The king, whose name was Little Steven, called his chief
advisors and asked that they present him with his official decree papers.
Those papers decreed, officially: *All giraffes are hereby forbidden from shipbuilding of any kind or sort,*
must complete all crosswordss in pen — not pencil — and are strictly prohibited from any further off-shore oil refining.

The king then stamped his decree and asked to be left alone for a while, so he
might have a nap, or a cucumber sandwich. However, the king's army was ordered
to travel up North to show the giraffes the stamped decree and end their semi-
lucrative endeavor. But when they finally arrived, the giraffes and their ships were
way gone. In fact, the giraffes had set sail a week before, toward America, knowing
that the king wished to do them in.

TYPES OF SAILING VESSELS

BARK   BARKENTINE   BRIGANTINE   BRIG

The giraffes knew this because they're smart, and have very good hearing when the wind is blowing
right. And so the giraffes soon reached America where they promptly lost their accents and invented
the American clipper ship that was to play such a pivotal role in the War of 1812.

And as you might have guessed, this story also illustrates why to this
day the Dutch flag is one-third blue — to symbolize the tears of the
Hollandnesh king who rejected the brilliant ships of the giraffes and
thus made the Netherlands the confusing place it is today.

GIRAFFES AND THEIR OPPONENTS, THE MONSTERS OF THE DEEP

Giraffes have traditionally had problematic relationships with the world's fierce sea monsters — the Giant Squid of the Lower Adriatic, the Gigantic Clam of the Red Sea, etc. — and the reasons are obvious: The giant sea creatures are jealous of the giraffes' dancing techniques and their sandwiches.

The battles between the giraffes, in their clipper ships, and the sea monsters are legendary. Take these three examples:

1. THE CLIPPER SHIP EDWARD RHYS-DAVIS BATTLES THE HUMONGOUS SAND WOMAN OF UPPER VOLTA

This took place in 1867, off the coast of Africa. Do not ask why the giraffes were sailing off the coast of Africa. I could tell you, but it would bring you to tears. The point is that they were there, and so was the Humongous Sand Woman of Upper Volta. Do not ask why the Humongous Sand Woman of Upper Volta was in the ocean, when she would probably be more comfortable in a dry climate, like a desert. The point, again, is that the giraffes and the Humongous Sand Woman of Upper Volta had a very fierce battle, which upset everyone, and left everyone involved very, very tired.

2. THE CLIPPER SHIP BELINDA RHYS-DAVIS BATTLES THE VERY FEARSOME AND LARGE HALF-LOBSTER-HALF-STARFISH

This battle happened in 1910, off the coast of Daytona Beach, Florida. Daytona Beach is a great place to buy a cool T-shirt, by the way. The shirt might say something like "Life Is a Party," or "Life Is Very Nice" or "Life Is Like Being at the Beach on a Nice Day." Anyhoo, this one day, the clipper ship Belinda Rhys-Davis came upon the Very Fearsome and Large Half-Lobster-Half-Starfish, whose real name was Eric Vratimos and was always looking for a fight. This battle didn't last very long, because Eric Vratimos isn't such a good fighter, and started crying when the giraffes messed up his hair.

3. THE CLIPPER SHIP TINA YOTHERS BATTLES THE INDESCRIBABLY INIMITABLE AND BIG DRIFTWOOD CREATURE OF THE BAY OF BENGALI

This just happened last week, so you probably read about it in the paper.

To make these simulations as accurate as possible, the sea creatures are being represented by plastic toys, and the giraffe clipper ships have been fashioned out of fig-oriented treats.

THE STORY OF JUANITA GROADMAN

Juanita Groadman was a simple giraffe girl with a love in her heart for zinc. Throughout her childhood the very mention of the word could send her into ecstatic joy. Whenever Mr. and Mrs. Groadman left the house and Juanita would find herself left to her own devices, she would run to her room and dream of zinc. As she grew, her family tried to replace this fixation with friends or boys, but Juanita was not to be dissuaded. It was zinc she loved! There was only one thing that could make Juanita stop thinking about the 30th element, and that was bridge building. Suspension, beam, truss — Juanita loved all types of bridges.

DID YOU KNOW?

A penny is 98% Zinc. That's why they're so crunchy!

ORES OF ZINC

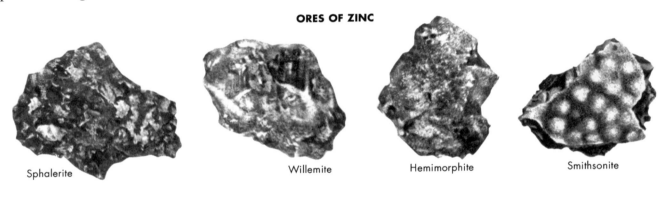

Sphalerite   Willemite   Hemimorphite   Smithsonite

Unfortunately, Juanita lived in the time before bridge-building instructional books for children — I, Dr. Doris Haggis-On-Whey, am almost finished with such a book myself — so the only way she could gain more knowledge about bridges was to ride her bike down to a builder's office and tug on every pantleg until someone would give her some answers. Most of the people there would ignore her, but eventually a man at the office, his name being Stuart Stewart, saw the potential in such an interested and motivated lass. Soon after, Juanita would be off every morning to the bakery or coffee shop, picking up something for her new friend. When she returned, Stuart Stewart would pat Juanita on the head. He'd say, "You'll be in the bridge building industry in no time!" Oh boy was he right! thought Juanita on her graduation day from the University of Bridgediers.

Being such a young and bright talent in the field, Juanita was recruited by many bridgemaking companies, but she knew she wanted nothing more than to help her own town build their very first bridge. Everyone in the town was so impressed with Juanita and her shiny yellow hard hat, her fancy rulers and notebooks, and her fantastic talk about floating towers and high tension beams.

But the help Juanita had was never very good. To be honest, she had the worst crew any bridge-builder ever had. Man, they were terrible. They only wanted to eat lunch, all day, and even then they ate it slowly. And you know what they were always eating? Hummus! Hummus is for losers.

So one day while Juanita was in the air, spinning the cables, another young giraffe, who was supposed to be operating the crane, dropped part of the road deck on Juanita. Why? Because he'd been eating too much hummus, and it had screwed up his brain, which is what hummus does to brains. (It does! All my studies say that the terrible smell associated with hummus is just an outward sign that it's messing with your very brain!) Anyhoo, Juanita was crushed entirely, hard hat and all. She was okay, but was thereafter much shorter.

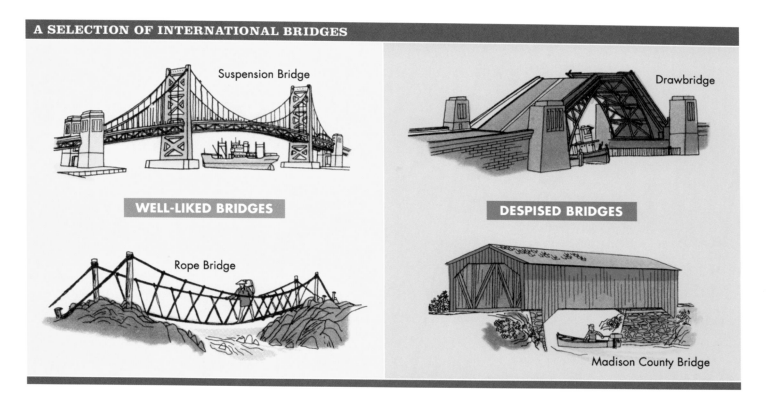

A SELECTION OF INTERNATIONAL BRIDGES

Suspension Bridge

Drawbridge

WELL-LIKED BRIDGES

DESPISED BRIDGES

Rope Bridge

Madison County Bridge

THE STORY OF TED "THEODORE" LOGAN, WHO CONSIDERED HIMSELF A FRIEND OF DESCARTES BUT WHO WAS NOT INVITED TO HIS WEDDING

In 1619, Rene Descartes, a bright, intelligent 23-years-young Frenchman, ran for seven hours in full medieval armor away from the battle he was supposed to be fighting for Prince Maurice of Nassau. He ran until he stumbled and fell into Ted Logan's prized artichoke garden.

Ted Logan was a prominent French giraffe and farmer and a lover of the ancient sport of jai-alai. Ted watched as Descartes hobbled around frantically on his newly sprained ankle and finally asked the man if he needed a place to rest. Descartes wound up spending two weeks with his new friend Ted Logan and found Ted to be equipped with a refreshingly bright mind. The two talked about everything from politics to aesthetics to the hats that women should wear, and as Descartes took leave of his friend they promised to correspond often.

JAI-ALAI, THE SPORT OF KINGS

When Descartes set down to write *Passions of the Soul*, many of his concepts of prenatal ideas were inspired by moonlight conversations he had with Ted. When Ted went fishing in the following spring, he invited Descartes along and taught him how. Soon after Descartes met his eventual wife Aaltje, he invited Ted to join them on their trip to Corsica. The times were sweet. But only two years later, when the Descartes family's wedding invitations were sent to the post, none were addressed to Ted.

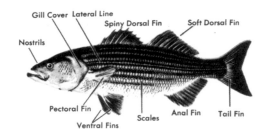
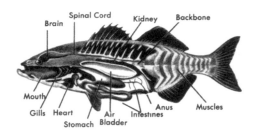

It was a large wedding and Ted was a likeable guy yet Descartes did not reserve a seat for him at his most joyous of days. Why was that? Was it something Ted wrote in an email? Ted went through all the messages he'd sent to Descartes, but couldn't find anything in particular that might have offended his friend. Did he forward too many jokes? Too many fund-raising emails from people he knew who were running in 5k Fun Runs? What was it?

If you have any insight, Ted would like you to email him: Ted@haggis-on-whey.com.

MOVE ALONG, READERS WHO ARE NOT GIRAFFES!

Hello. Sorry for the extremely small type here. But we had to tell you things we couldn't have the giraffes reading, and everyone knows that giraffes can't read very small type, and they certainly can't read anything in blue type, ever. So we're safe. Do you feel safe? Good. We do, too. There are some things we wanted you to know about our subjects that would either hurt the feelings of giraffes or endanger our own lives. First of all, giraffes sometimes smell very bad. They have been told this a few times by Mr. Haggis-on-Whey and myself, but they don't seem to get the message. What do they smell like, you ask? They smell like pastrami. Maybe you're a big fan of pastrami, and you like everything to smell like this kind of lunchmeat. If so, you're welcome to smell giraffes, up close, all you want. But personally, we like only one thing to smell like pastrami, and that's pastrami. When do giraffes smell like pastrami? In these instances: 1) After taking hot tubs; 2) After doing some very intense origami; 3) Before reading books about oceans. Now, for some giraffes, these situations happen very often, which means, yes: they frequently smell like pastrami. And it's not even good pastrami. It's the odor of a very cheap pastrami. Not the deli kind, that you'd order by the pound, and it would be dry and spicy. No, this is a wet, stinky pastrami that you get in a plastic package, all the round slices laid out like playing cards. Imagine the smell of this pastrami. Now imagine a whole huge mammal covered in it, head to toe. Now imagine that instead of actually being covered in it, head to toe, it only smelled like this huge mammal was covered in it. Now you know what it's like to be around a giraffe after some origami. The other thing I wanted to mention is that Marcus isn't really one of the best-looking giraffes. (See p. 23). You probably noticed this. He's really sort of goofy-looking, if you ask me—he's nowhere near as handsome as Giacomo (p.27) or Gunther (p. 29). But Marcus overheard that we were writing a book, and that there would be some pages with good-looking giraffes pictured, and you know what he did? He came to our house! He flew from Terre Haute, Indiana, all the way to our cottage in Crumpets-under-Kilts. He just showed up one day, and rang the bell. Actually, he didn't ring the bell, because the bell was broken. He knocked on the door, loudly. No, he didn't knock on the door, come to think of it. The door was being replaced that week, so there was no door. What did he do, anyway? I'm going to ask Mr. Haggis-on-Whey. Okay, now I'm back. I just asked my husband and he remembered that Marcus had come around to the back of the house, where Mr. and I were sunbathing while wearing eggplants. This is something we do often, because it helps bring universal energy into our brains and feet, the two most important parts of one's person. So we were there, in the back, on our hammocks, bringing the energy of the universe into our brains and our feet, when something literally blotted out the sun! Really! We looked up, thinking it was a visitor from Sector 7 or possibly a Fhumoud!-Fuba, but it wasn't either of those things. It was Marcus. "Hey guys," he said. "I hear you're putting together some kind of book with pictures of great-looking guys like me." I answered that in fact we were putting together a reference book about his species, to be studied by discerning scholars around the world. Inside this book, I admitted, would be a few pictures of the most attractive giraffes. "So where do I sign up?" he asked. "How much do I get paid?" he said. He was a very annoying giraffe. He had a bunch of pictures with him. I asked what the pictures were. He said they were pictures of himself, in many different poses and with many different outfits. In a few pictures, he was wearing a cape, like a superhero. Mr. Haggis-on-Whey and myself found these photos, and Marcus himself, very amusing. He was a young giraffe who had traveled by plane 6,000 miles to come and show us pictures of himself wearing a cape. This cape, I should mention, was made of polyester, a material that everyone knows doesn't fly. Cotton and wool fly, and Gore-Tex flies, but polyester doesn't fly, never has. But perhaps Marcus wasn't planning to actually fly. So we had poor Marcus in for tea and cucumber sandwiches, which he ate very happily. I'm not sure why I told you that whole story. Oh, now I know. The main thing I wanted to talk to you about was how giraffes will play piano when they come over to visit. And Marcus was certainly giraffe-like in this regard! You know what I'm talking about. I'm talking about the people who can't stay away from a piano, even though they've never taken a lesson in their life. Okay, let's say there's a piano in the room. It's just there, and no one usually plays it, because it's so out of tune that when played, it sounds like someone stepped on a seal. But in comes the giraffe, and the giraffe has never learned to play a note. But what does he do? He heads straight for the piano bench! He sits down. He opens the piano lid, the thing that protects the keys, and he starts hitting the keys. You know what he's doing? He's touching the keys, thinking that he'll magically start to know what he's doing. But of course he doesn't know. He'll just sit there, in your living room, after eating eleven cucumber sandwiches, and he'll be tapping on your piano that sounds like a seal. Humming to himself! And I have to tell you, as bad as some giraffes smell—like pastrami—they're much worse when they hum. They hum like pastrami would hum, if it could hum, which it can't anymore, ever since Senator Alan Simpson of Wyoming passed a law against it, thank god. This is what Marcus did when he came over with his pictures of himself in a cape, he hacked away at the piano and he hummed like pastrami. We finally got him to leave by jumping up and down on the floor, which all giraffes hate. If you ever want to get a giraffe to leave your house, just jump up and down. But jump in place! Don't move all around like you're on a pogo stick! Just jump up and down in place, and the giraffe will leave within a few minutes. Something about the jumping just bugs them. Speaking of bugging people, did I ever tell you about my brother Cecil? Oooh boy, that's someone who could really get on your nerves. Have you met him? You haven't? Well, you're lucky. He's a year older than I, Dr. Doris Haggis-On-Whey, am and he still thinks he's my big brother, even though neither of us is a teenager anymore. When I see him, he still gives me what in my day we used to call 'gomble-smacks.' What is a gomble-smack, you ask? I will tell you, but you must promise never to do this to one of your own siblings or friends. To give someone a gomble-smack, you stand behind them, and you do two things at the same time. 1) You push your knee into the back of their knee, causing them to slightly lose their balance. 2) While doing this, you are also tickling either side of their waist. If they are ticklish, when you do these two things at the same time, the recipient of a gomble-smack will leap at least a foot in the air and shriek. Well, my brother Cecil still does this to me, which is not an appropiate thing to do to a world-famous scientist and explorer like myself. So, where were we? We were telling you all the facts about giraffes that they wouldn't want us telling you. You want to know a very interesting thing? Giraffes are very bad at four-square. It's kind of strange, because they're very good at tetherball and bocce ball. But yes, it's true, they're not very good at four square. They lose every time. The second they get back into Square Four, they get knocked out again. Almost never do they make it all the way to Square One. And it has nothing to do with the fact that they have hooves, and not hands. And it's not because, when standing on their hind legs, they can get to be as much as thirty feet tall. No, it's more about their shot-placement. They can't find the corners. This is why they're also not very good at billiards. Okay, I guesss that's all we wanted to say here, in this small type that giraffes can't read.

-Dr. Doris Haggis-On-Whey

NOTHING TO SEE HERE!

GIRAFFES ARE SUSPICIOUS OF YELLOW BOWS

THE STORY OF THE GIRAFFES' FEUD WITH THE ASSISTANT SECRETARY OF AGRICULTURE, DONALD J. PENDELTON

The year was 1953 and there was a group of giraffe-farmers who grew red onions in Hotlanta! They had done very well for themselves. They had taken over the whole Hotlanta! red-onion business and successfully driven out all competition. Donald J. Pendelton was a newly appointed Assistant Secretary of Agriculture who felt he had something to prove. Donald J. Pendelton, or D.J., as it appeared in his fourth-grade yearbook, first noticed a problem when, at the age of 10, his entire body began to grow into adulthood with the exception of his right leg.

GIRAFFES HARD AT WORK IN THEIR NATURAL ENVIRONMENT: THE ONION FIELDS OF HOTLANTA!

By the age of 14, Donald J. Pendelton — or "Bucky" as it appears in his eighth-grade yearbook — stood five-foot-eight on his left leg and four-foot-six on his right. Thus it was very obvious to everyone why Donald J. Pendelton would have such a personal problem with the giraffe onion farmers, who were, of course, tall. The giraffes were in the proverbial pickle. How did all this get resolved? Well, you can just ask "Bucky" about that, can't you? He's right there, on the right-hand page. Ask him! (The answer is on page 62. Or actually, it's not.)

This drawing was done by *sanitary* monks.

Can I vent for a second, here? I needed someone to draw me a picture of the Sec. of Agriculture, so I went to the monastery. Well, guess what I found there? A bunch of monks who were unclean! I was flabbergasted! I said, How are you guys going to draw an accurate rendering of Pendleton when your hands are dirty, and your legs are covered in jelly and rabbit fur? They had no explanation. So I went to the Monk Union, Local 45-8, and told them I was looking for some sanitary monks to give me a drawing. They said, "Oh, a sanitary monk? We don't have those types anymore. Try Chile." So I had to go all the way to Chile — I had some movies I had to return to a Blockbuster there, so it was cool — to find a clean monk. But it was worth it. They're really clean there! Boy, are they clean.

— Dr. H-O-W

HOW TO MAKE A BREAD SANDWICH

There's almost no reason to bother telling you how to make a bread sandwich, because chances are you will not succeed. Bread sandwiches are usually assembled by teams of Austrian dental students, using stainless steel tools and also a complicated system of weights and pulleys. You won't be able to do it! So why try? You could hurt yourself. You could bring injury and ruin to those around you. You could even damage the upholstery or anger your parents and relatives. Nevertheless, because we are reckless, we will offer to you four of the most popular recipes for bread sandwiches, the favored food of giraffes of the greater Terre Haute, Indiana, area.

THE SANDWICH OF HORATIO	Two slices of Jewish rye bread One slice of white bread Three slices of pumpernickel (served on the side) Three small garden weeds (to be stapled together and thrown WEST) One slice of sourdough (very thin!) *- Mix together alphabetically and eat in reverse order*
THE SANDWICH OF SANDRA & GUADALUPE	Four slices of Russian rye (not Jewish rye!) Two slices of Jewish rye (miniature-size) 1/4 lb Swedish wasa bread (unbleached) 3 strips of foccacia (no garlic!) 1 square foot of ficelli *- Eat while thinking about older women in white sweatsuits*
THE SANDWICH OF CRAZY MARION AND PECULIAR HECTOR	3 lbs of sweetbreads One kaiser roll Large glass of water *- Eat in a dark room, surrounded by puppies*
THE SANDWICH WHICH HAS NO NAME	Two slices of rye bread One slice of white bread Three slices of pumpernickel (served on the side) Three small garden weeds (to be stapled together and thrown EAST or NORTHEAST) One slice of sourdough (not as thin as Horatio's!) *- Eat all at once, with eyes closed and arms crossed. Pout!*

NATURE'S CRUELEST JOKE:
THE MINIATURE GIRAFFE

I realize that some of the information we've been giving you is light-hearted and enjoyable to read. Well, now I must discuss with you something serious. Something very serious. It's so serious that I want you to take off any pink or light-blue clothing, and I want you to cover your ears, so there are no distractions. Have you done this? Why are you so slow at everything that matters?

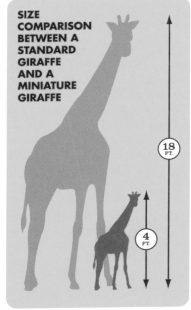

We must stop the exploitation of miniature giraffes! You have seen these poor creatures. They are just like regular giraffes, except that whereas regular giraffes are very tall, these miniature giraffes are — you guessed it — not as tall.

But because many people find them to be "cute," they have been used in many ways that are not dignified. Take, for example, their inclusion in many professional baseball teams of the early 20th century. Because giraffes are naturally good bunters and third basemen, it would follow that a *miniature* giraffe would be even better! And so they were recruited to play baseball, and were paid lots of money for their efforts. This wasn't fair to anyone.

Nowadays, they are kept as pets. These animals, with IQs in the 400s, are being told to "sit" and "roll over" and "lick my face and bark!" This is an outrage!

Please write to your local senator or president and tell them that you won't buy any more of their pastrami or car stereos or tanks unless they do something about this. Now!

DEAR SENATOR/REPRESENTATIVE _____,
(CIRCLE ONE)

All this miniature-giraffe business has to stop! Look at these poor animals! They don't want to be serving drinks at barbecues and being ridden by toddlers, like miniature camels! As my elected representive, I urge you to pass some very good laws to outlaw the sale and exploitation of miniature giraffes. If you pass such a law, I promise to wave to you when you drive by next Fourth of July. If you do not pass such a law, I will stick my thumb on my nose and wave my fingers at you. This will indicate that I am not happy with you, elected person!

Sincerely,

_____   _____   _____
PRINT NAME   WEIGHT   FAVORITE TRADE PUBLICATION

_____   _____   _____
ADDRESS   FAVORITE SKATING STAR   HAT SIZE

That giraffes won't drink milk through a straw (unless you ask them to, while wearing a hockey mask)?

That when giraffes see campfires, they laugh hysterically?

DID YOU KNOW?

That giraffes love to eat iced oatmeal cookies, but will only do so if they have been left out on the counter for two days, thus making them chewy? Yes, I guess you already knew this.

That giraffes invented plastic? No, not plastic — latex. My bad. Still, though, isn't that amazing?

HOW DID THE GIRAFFES COME TO BE SUCH GOOD FRIENDS WITH THE APPALACHIAN WHITE OWL?

It does seem odd that such charming and socially adept creatures as the giraffes should bother with a loner like the Appalachian white owl. But then again, giraffes are known to be peculiar on occasion. Did you know six giraffes once treaded water in the ocean for sixty-eight hours straight just to prove the local Kiwanas club wrong?

Anyway, a long time ago — "due to a budget crisis" — the Greater Atlanta Giraffe Historical Society were forced to reenact their PBS Lewis and Clark video trilogy in the factually inaccurate Appalachian mountains. Well, needless to say, the giraffes ran into a series of problems, none much fatiguing than the week they spent trying to make the Allegheny Plateau look vaguely like the Lolo Pass through the Bitterroot Mountains. The Appalachian white owl, seeing the giraffes in such a predicament and knowing the poor funding PBS receives, decided to do his part to aid the giraffes. "Make it a character-driven drama rather than historically centralized," said the owl from a nearby pear tree. "And throw in some trick photography." The owl had saved the movie and the careers of all involved!

Regrettably the film received no awards and was largely ignored, but a cameraman was asked about the rights to the white owl story when he told the anecdote to a prominent Hollywood type. That's why to this day no matter what the white owl can expect cornucopia for Easter from his good friends the giraffes.

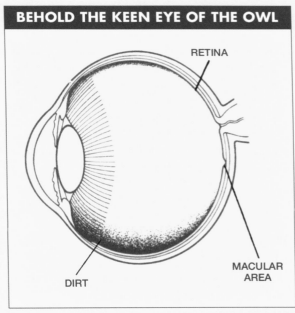

BEHOLD THE KEEN EYE OF THE OWL

RETINA

MACULAR AREA

DIRT

Well, that's all we have for you now, regarding giraffes and Madagascar. We hope you have learned a lot, and have finally replaced all that nonsense which had previously filled your head. But how can we be sure that you've digested all the knowledge included in this beautiful book? The fact is, we can't. We can watch you with one of our many orbiting surveillance satellites, sure, but even then, the audio is not so good. So perhaps you should write to us. Or make a xerox of your left arm and send it to us. Or send us your toenail clippings — Benny has quite a collection, and as of right now, has no examples of such foot-oriented detritus from the following states: Hawaii, Oklahoma, Iowa, Maryland, Georgia, Missouri, Oregon, and North Dakota. (If you are from South Dakota, *please do not send toenail clippings!* We have plenty already from you people.) Somehow enclosed in this book is an envelope, with a post office box we are currently using. Put something in this envelope, add a stamp, and put it not in the toaster, but in the mailbox. Mailboxes are usually blue. Please try not to screw this up. When you drop your missive in the box, be assured that all of this mail will be eventually forwarded to our location on the Isle of Air, and we will read your correspondence while sitting in our garden, eating cucumber sandwiches and hoping not to be interrupted by piano-playing giraffes. We hope to hear from you soon. Do not send hummus.

Your expecting givers of wisdom,
Dr. Doris and Mr. Benny Haggis-On-Whey

POSSIBLE UPCOMING TITLES FROM THE H-O-W SERIES*

Neptune: Our Most Greenish-Yellow Planet

The Post Office: Magic and Mystery

How and Why Wood Thinks

Basic Spacecraft Design and Operation

Kittens: Can We Prevent Them from Becoming Cats?

Fraud! Why You Should Not Use a Lunch Box

Cardboard: Issues and Ethics

Books: Should We Read Them or Use Them to Make Shoes?

The Best Clothing for Capybaras

What Are Capybaras Thinking?

Why Do Capybaras Find Everything We Say So Amusing?

Really, What Is Their Problem?

Thrones for Every Season

The H-O-W English-to-Giant Squid Dictionary

Plants: Where Are They Now?

When Cats Stop Painting

People and Birds, and the Separate and Different Lives They Lead

112 Ways to Kick Start Your Felt Collection

Socialism Calling, Will You Accept the Charges?

Why We're All Usually Sleepy

The Truth About Capes

Trends: On Their Way Out?

Where Pets Go to Cry

Garbage Then, Now, and Here to Stay

Permanent Markers: Are They?

Plaid vs. Corduroy, When Will the Fighting End?

The Things They Dropped

Glass, Roman Generals, and Welding

Inside the Minds of Jamaica's Striped Animals

Stuff around the House and How Much It Could Be Worth

The De-mystification of the Orient

French Limericks

Palindromes — In Outer Space!

The Harmonium: Music's Next Guitar

The ABCs of Bilateral International Infrastructure Insurance Fraud Investigations

Where Boys Dance When It's Quiet

*subject to change

Note: The guns being held in the picture above are not real guns. Dr. Doris and Benny Haggis-On-Whey do not like guns, and have never fired one. Holding these guns was the idea of a man named Frederico, who left the country shortly after this photo was taken.

ABOUT THE AUTHORS

Dr. Doris Haggis-On-Whey has seventeen degrees from eighteen institutions of higher learning. She is a world-renowned and much-feared expert on just about everything. With her husband Benny, she has traveled the world many times over, and has learned about all aspects of life, including outer space and food, first-hand. She has written or will soon write over 147 books about subjects such as: Fiberglass Insulation, Wolverines, Hallways, Neptune, Dogs Who Play Poker, Tangelos, How and Why Wood Thinks, Giant Squids, The Post Office, Thrones, Spacecraft Design and Operation, Lunch Boxes, Cardboard, and The Best Clothing for Capybaras.

Benny is the husband of Dr. Doris Haggis-On-Whey, and enjoys putting on his socks.

ABOUT THE DESIGNERS

Mark Wasserman and Irene Ng have recently been employed by Dr. Haggis-On-Whey to help in designing the HOW series of books. They live in San Francisco, thankfully very far away from the awful temper of Dr. Haggis-On-Whey, who of course lives in upper Scotland, on the Isle of Air.

Research assistance has been provided by the de la Manzana brothers, and by Dave and Toph Eggers.